With Love

and

Peace

Acknowledgments

To all my friends and family who willingly gave of their time to edit the stories of my twelve books; patiently taught me computer jargon; shared their computer skills with InDesign and Photoshop; and guided me through the copyright, ISBN and barcode maze. I couldn't have done it without you.

With God in Mind

Individual works written between 1990 to 2009.

All Bible quotes were taken from
"The Companion Bible," The Authorized
Version of 1611 with Structures
and Critical Explanatory, Kregel
Publications.

Front Cover: A Photo of the ocean at
Marina State Park in Marina, California

ISBN: 978-1-947573-08-6

Library of Congress Catalog Card Number: 2017950599

The Carolee Collectables
Printed in the United States of America
www.crystalsforkids.org

Carolee O'Neill
http://books2c4kids.com

Index

Titles

Index

Titles

Dedication

To those who encouraged me to go forward with my life in spite of adversity. To those who so willing shared their gifts of talent and love. I have been blessed to have had the privilege of being in their care as they guided me toward my eternal home.

Blessings Always,

Carolee

With God in Mind

by Carolee O'Neill

To:

_____

_____

From:

_____

_____

Catch My Eye, Lord

Ps 74:16. The day is Thine, the night also is Thine: Thou hast prepared the light and the sun. Thou hast set all the borders of the earth: Thou hast made summer and winter.

Did you see it? It caught me by surprise when I glanced out of the window. This one began at dawn.

Dull crystals filled the air, held in suspension by an unknown. No sunlight struck the crystal-like shapes to brighten the images that they portrayed on the nearby trees and roofs.

The lawns joined their obscurity with a thick frost that looked like the tangled silver hair of an elderly person who awaited morning care.

Held in the moment by curiosity, I continued to gaze.

Another one of His paintings—the Lord intended the day to begin this way. How long will He hold the world in this scene, a moment—an hour?

Instantly the cloud cover opened. Crystals burst into sparkling facets. Light streaked across the land to soften the brittleness of that previous aged image. A heavenly tingle, warm and consoling, engulfed my being. As the vision unfolded, I realized that God had blessed me with another day—at least these moments. And yet, I continued to take every one for granted, living as though there were endless tomorrows.

Respectfully, I thought of the work that He intended, not my likely plan.

Open my mind to the depths of your word dear Father, so that my life will be filled with your truth, with more thanksgiving for my blessings, and with fewer thoughts of my list of doings.

Cradle me in your arms this day, so I'll feel safe to fulfill your desires. And if it be your will, one more day will be mine and I may be privileged to see another one of your paintings.

With God in Mind

At the dawn of a new day, I will once again ponder your dream of the seeds that need to be planted. As I do, perhaps an imaging of your smile will be forthcoming.

Then my heart will thrill to the heavens, for by chance you might feel my job had been well done.

Acceptance

Lk: 9:48. And said unto them, "Whosoever shall receive this child in My name receiveth Me: and whosoever shall receive Me receiveth Him that sent Me: of he that is least among you all, the same shall be great."

With God in Mind

Marty jingled the few coins in his pocket. It was his severance pay, so to speak, an insult. As though so little could pay for what he had endured the last five years. Impatiently he watched as the prison guard fumbled with the keys on the large, steel ring. The guard grunted when the tumblers finally responded to the pressure, and gave up their grip on the massive prison lock. Pulling back on the iron barred gate, the sound of steel rubbing against steel penetrated the silence. Marty's long awaited freedom was before him.

The red-faced guard stood sway-backed with a plentiful stomach that hovered over his belt. He sneered as he stepped aside. "We'll see how long it is before you're back in here. You're no better than the rest of these guys, Marty. You just think you are."

The snide remark caused Marty's stomach to sour and his clean shaven face to twist with pain. He wanted to lash out with all of his pent-up anger, but knew that wouldn't be smart. What would it accomplish—more wasted years? Clearly he remembered his slender body being shoved through the passageways five years ago and the sound of the steel gate slamming behind him. He had been incarcerated for a crime that he hadn't committed, but no one cared or listened to his plea.

As he began his lonely journey down the deserted road, Marty wondered what would happen to him. He had been stripped of everything, his job, his family, his sense of decency. Today he faced a different world, a world that shunned convicts, even if they were innocent.

How am I supposed to live? Who will give an x-con a job? Let's face it. Nobody really cares what happens to me. All I know is that I need to get as far away from this place as possible. Even if it means walking until I drop.

Suddenly something brushed against his pant leg. Then he heard a muffled, clacking sound like stone hitting against stone. He looked down. A rock the size of a golf ball lay on the pavement. A crumpled piece of paper was wrapped around it and attached with a rubber band. He picked it up and removed the paper.

Printed in bold letters was, "Whoever finds this—I love you!"

Marty laughed sarcastically, "You've got to be kidding. Who'd pull a stupid prank like this? Well, it's not funny."

He took a couple of steps forward, paused, and looked at the note again. His anger kindled, he hurled the rock and the paper to the ground. The rock bounced again and again like a stone skipping across water. The paper floated on a tender breeze, as though suspended in time.

"Some nut thinks he can solve the world's problems with the word love."

He began to turn in circles, mocking the words on the paper as he delivered his hurtful message to the wind. "It's no use. There's nothing left to save. You're wasting your rocks."

Silence was the only response.

"Why don't you answer me?" he shouted passionately as his burden choked his words. "Are you afraid to? Do you think I'm going to kill you, because I just got out of that place? Well, I wasn't guilty.

"No! I wasn't guilty, but they stuck me in there for five years, anyway.

"Now I have nothing—nothing left."

Marty fought back the tears as he spoke, but finally gave way to his despair. Heaviness filled his body. Slowly he sank from the weight of his anguish, finding a resting place on the curb. He sat there for what seemed hours, crying and sobbing.

He began to fumble through one pocket after another, looking for a handkerchief, but found none.

A soft touch on his shoulder revealed a child with saddened eyes, holding a tissue. "It's OK, Mister," she said with a gentle smile on her lips. "I love you, anyway."

A Conversation with God

Mt: 6:6 But thou, when thou prayest, enter into
thy closet, and when thou hast shut thy door,
pray to thy Father which is in secret; and thy
Father which seeth in secret shall reward thee
openly.

With God in Mind

Good Morning Father,

Yes, it's me again. Looks like I made it through another night with a few ah-ha's to boot. I guess you can't get my attention during the day, so you have to do it when I'm finally still. It's too bad that I get so busy with tasks that I forget to talk to you or read a few verses from the Bible.

I'll try harder today.

Do you ever feel bogged down with chores and stuff? The Bible says we're made in your image, so I can't help wonder about that. There are so many of us to keep track of. We're like a zillion ants on honey, bent on moving the food into a hole. That helps us side-step your memory, and then we forget how much you love us. You've done so much for me Father. If I remember you half as much as you remember me—wouldn't that be something! Now there's a job for me.

I'll try harder today.

Will you give the Holy Spirit and my guardian angel a message for me? Tell them that if I'm not listening, they have my permission to make me misplace something, forget something or drop something. Then you'll be the one who pops into my head.

The way I have it figured, with the Holy Spirit beside me and my guardian angel losing my stuff, I'm sure to make some improvements.

I'll try harder today Father.

Talk to you later.

By the way,

I love you!

Surely God Smiles

Mt. 25:21. "Well done, thou good and
faithful servant."

With God in Mind

My Dearest Grandson,

The Holidays are past as I sit with your letter in hand from Iraq, thinking about the future. As you continue to glorify God with your actions, the war persists both here and in Iraq. The only difference is that in our country bombs and bullets have been replaced by the actions of protesters who argue that they are "right." Those against the war stand on street corners waving signs that read, "Stop the war, now"—"Bring our troops home"—"We don't belong in Iraq." Those that are for the war shout "Remember 9/11"—"They killed our people"—"We must stop the terrorists before they bring the war to our shores." Still others say there are similarities with the Vietnam War. They fear that our troops do not feel appreciated.

Nevertheless, no matter what the cause, our men and women are making sacrifices so that we can be free to do as we wish.

Remember when you were a little boy, parents gathered along the sidelines of a game. For the sake of being right, disapprovals were shouted by families and friends with red-faced anger as the children listened in disbelief. It's no different today with the pros and cons. Controlled by their cause, they seem equally blind to the possibility that they are both "right." But it's not a game that we are talking about—it is a war.

American's are shouting their disapproval while our men and women are fighting at war. The cause seems to be playing ball with the enemy.

Surely God cries when he sees how easily our nation has been divided; how easily we have been distracted from our mission.

You and many like you have spoken words that haven't been heard.

"Don't believe what the media says about the war. They don't know what they are talking about."

"Is it important that we are in Iraq. These people are taking part in some freedoms that they have never had before."

In Iraq, the place you call home, is a bombed-out garage. You've endured temperatures that have soared to 140 degrees, robbing you of your strength. The sands of the desert have been your living room and your bathroom, providing no comforts of home, no way to cleanse your body or wash your hands. Men and women whom you have grown to respect have died in your arms. You have watched as children barter for nickels with gum and have seen people being forced to live in broken buildings heaped with garbage.

Despite these adversities, you and many like you have continued to embrace a cause that will bring about a better world, a peaceful nation. Your sacrifices have been great.

We, who have only heard of war, can not fathom the conditions of which you speak nor understand poverty in this form.

In the shadows of our domestic war, our street people rummage through garbage for food, warm their hands over fires in trash cans, wander the night for a box to sleep in or a doorway to capture a little warmth. But they are not among the activists, even though they are the ones who understand the war that you are fighting, the poverty that you see. Perhaps the pros and cons are the things that we do to void ourselves of the actuality of war—like not seeing the poor among us.

Surely God cries as He looks upon His children's weary spirits.

Your words about the children in Iraq have rekindled a memory that happened long before your time, during World War ll. At best it is a poor comparison to what you are experiencing. However, it is an actual event seen through the eyes of a child.

I remember sitting at my desk in the second grade. Suddenly, sirens blared from the town hall. I looked skyward as though I could see the bombs dropping.

Carolee O'Neill

Was it a real air raid this time or another
warning of that possibility? Sitting frozen in my
seat, I watched as the nuns scurried to gather us
together. Sister pulled me from my desk, as she
said. "It's only a drill, children. But you must hurry;
we have to get to the basement as soon as possible."

In silence, the first, second and third graders
ran down the stairs to the basement, never turning to
look back. The rustle of habits—the sound of rosary
beads clacked in the rush. Once in the basement
Sister sorted us by class; she needed to know where
everyone was, just in case. Our backs were pressed
against the wall of the boiler, as we stood lined up.
None of us moved. We listened to the up and down
of the siren's melody as it continued to announce
our possible doom. Eyes were turned skyward, we
stood, terrified.

With God in Mind

Fear ravaged my body as my heart banged in my chest. Would there be real bombs this time? I was sure that I could hear their whistles. Then the siren slowly whined down, but my heart continued to pound. I didn't believe the alarm's silence. I continued to listen.

Surely God must smile when He looks upon all of the children that our men and women are trying to protect.

Will He not say, "Well done, thou good and faithful servant." Mt. 25:21.

With all the adversity, I still hear joy in your words. You wrote a joke—you signed your letter with a Latin phrase meaning, "Seize the Moment."

Carolee O'Neill

You, my dearest, have given me the gift

of freedom, the gift of hope—you have given

me the gift of love.

I love you,

Grandma

Published 2006: Together in Faith.

The Tides of Life

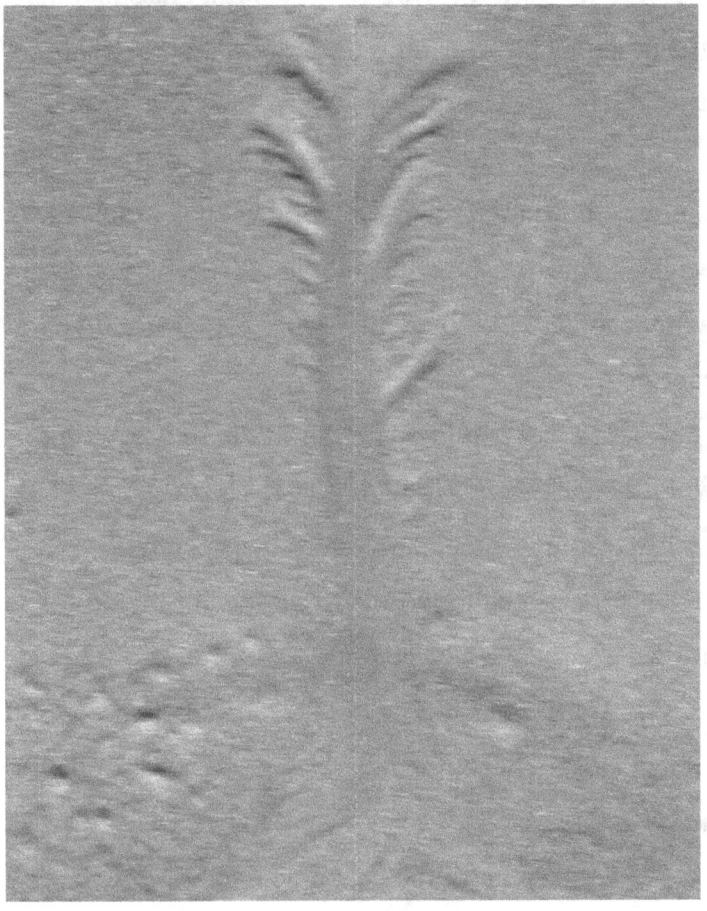

Actual Photo of a Sand Sculpture.
There was nothing on the beach to
form these, except the motion of the sea.

Carolee O'Neill

I look to the horizon for a vibrant sunset.
I look to the earth for flowers to bloom, grass that's
green, mountains touching the sky and valleys that
dip deep to caress a river.

I look toward the ocean as I walk on its
shores. Gulls caw as they skim above the crest of the
waves. Wings flash white and black—necks stretched
with a readied bill. Suddenly wings fold into a dive to
capture their prey.

The sky is alive with the flutter of black and
white as nature joins in their quest. The ocean replies
with splashing waters that hinder their pursuit.

The sea continues its rhythm, churning to
draw the sand to itself—smooth, yet firm.

A gull floats on the waves, seen and unseen.
Its head tosses back, the meal devoured before a new
hunt begins.

Footprints fill the beach where the water has
left its mark. People pass at a brisk pace with no
glance toward the sea. Others run a straight path to
where I do not know. Still others sit back from the
breakers to read the newspaper or bathe in the sun. A

few souls close their eyes to listen to the music of the tide, to drink in the peace of its tempo, and feel the salty mist on their skin. Others interrupt that peace with chatter when they pass.

My footsteps are closer to the water now. The crashing sounds louder, the sand softer.

Something catches my eye as I look down. The image is visible, the likeness of a tree. Had man created this sand sculpture? It must be so—but it's so perfect.

No, my spirit whispers, man could not design something this remarkable.

How could this be—this imprint in the "sand?" Would the answer be forthcoming?

My eyes have never beheld a
phenomenon such as this Father.

Then more sculptures appear, each more perfect than the last. Many are joined by their bases, bottom to top. A steady stream of water washes deep into their centers before flowing back to the sea. Several groups of five or six are coupled, yet each with enough room to blossom. A forest lies beneath my feet with feathery boarders, a tropical flair—wet, soft, and vulnerable to the tide.

I look again to the ocean, and hear it thunder your love for us; I thrill when the sea lingers to soothe the sculptures, like the gentle touch of a lover.

And then the water trickles back to its fullness.

Thus the sea continues its endless tempo, a journey of comings and goings.

Deep in my soul I discern your mighty hand joins the calm of the sea with the power of the surf to make these delicate sculptures.

Are they made for us as a tiny glimpse into the heaven that awaits us?

You are present in all things—the sea, the sunset, the earth, in man—even in these precious imprints in the sand.

With God in Mind

My eyes drift toward the setting sun.
Another day is almost gone, unknown for the
secrets it holds.

The tides of time are absent from our minds.

We go forth, unaware of our own measure
of your love in our souls.

With surety, your love will bring us back to
you someday just like the water trickles through the
sculptures and returns to the sea.

Thank you Father.

My eyes have never beheld
a phenomenon such as this.

Carolee O'Neill

Another Type of Sand Sculpture

Notice background.

We Need Some Help
Down Here, Lord

I Peter: Chapter 5, 6 – 10: Humble yourselves therefore under the mighty hand of God, that He may exalt you in due time: Casting all your care upon Him; for He careth for you. Be sober, be vigilant; because your adversary the devil, as a roaring lion, walketh about, seeking whom he may devour: Whom resist stedfast in the faith, knowing that the same afflictions are accomplished in your brethren that are in the world. But the God of all grace, Who hath called us unto His eternal glory by Christ Jesus, after that ye have suffered a while, make you perfect, stablish, strengthen, settle you.

Where did everybody go? The parents, I mean. They seemed to have disappeared into places that I know little about. They pass through invisible walls of busy-ness to hide for the day. They drive with cell-phones to their ears as they rush to their walls and shuffle papers for a buck.

Upon arriving at work, machines hum a tune that keep them entranced with stacks of papers. Associates gather at the copy machine, the elevator, and the lunchroom with coffee in hand. Walls become alive with high and low pitched chatter that bounces into the realms of boredom.

It has been asked, "What would the walls say, if they could talk?"

"Gibberish! Gibberish!" they'd say. "We have better lives than they. Our walls are smooth, solid and we know where we stand. We don't traipse around with nothingness on our minds. We tend to our little walls and shelves that hold their bedlam of mindlessness."

The workers glanced randomly at the clock as it counted their seconds—was it time to leave yet? Without a doubt, each tick pushed their awareness of eternity out of the present and far into the future. Office phones rang throughout their impersonal space, gathering sounds from cubicles, side offices and the concealed cell phones. Less important positions added the clicking of computer keys, and the sound of coins, dropping into the pop or coffee machine.

People joined their walls with a need to chat—tell a joke, and they stayed longer than expected.

Carolee O'Neill

They are late getting back to their home

walls. Upon entering, they hear the kenneled dog

whine to be released. Anxious for relief he bounds

toward the door, rear legs overtaking front.

Cartoons blared from the living room, announcing

another presence. Because the hour is late, a

substitute supper of fast-food will be prepared. No

one offers a blessing or gives thanks for the meal.

No one comes to the table to share their day,

television captures that time. Bedtime will come

soon enough with a reminder that tomorrow will be

the same.

We need some help down here, Lord!

The children vanish into their own walls.

They are learning by example. Their custody has

been entrusted to strangers who they will get to

know better than their parents. Born with an

abundance of trust, their minds are easily filled with

lessons on what they should and shouldn't do, and

on how to like or dislike others and themselves. The

lessons go on to reveal that saying *thank you* isn't

considered *cool*. The walls groan from the

propaganda and redundancies.

Being shaped like play-dough, the children

learn to want more *stuff*, presuming that it will be

a good substitute for Mom or Dad. Surely, *things*

will make them happy, and will help them *fit in*

with their friends.

At school, the clock above the chalkboard

ticks the children's assumed eternal seconds. The

children pay no attention. Their young minds are

imprisoned by the excitement of things promised

in a mysterious place called the "Web." The

information age will be their god every day, both

boring and delighting them. Technology with its

endless robotic chores will imprison their minds.

We need some help down here, Lord!

Grandparents chisel holes in their walls to

peer at the family. They silently voice their

disapproval of the happenings, but never share the

consequences they foresee. That would be

interfering, which may cause the family to think

less of them. Worse yet, their wisdom could be

criticized. With self-appointed authority, they

attempt to set examples that will arrive too late.

When their efforts gain no acknowledgement, they

buy gifts for the family carefully wrapped in guilt.

The happenings of the day had to scurry to

keep pace with their remaining time, because their

clock ticks faster than the rest. Regrettably, each

tick sounded a dissonant chord to remind them of

their impending death.

In spite of this they procrastinated,

sidestepping responsibility for the family. The

myriad of daily medications had fogged their

awareness of these events, they said. Certainly, their

age or lack of energy was to blame.

We need some help down here, Lord!

The behavior continues.

Clocks stop.

Some mourn briefly.

Time is gone.

Surely, we need some help down here, Lord!

Carolee O'Neill

Beloved

From David: 1932 – 2001

to Carolee

I am the chosen envoy.

Not because of my fragrance

nor my discernible beauty. But that you have

observed my essence as I grow and blossom,

unfolding one petal at a time. Each moment we

may celebrate

that which lies veiled within. When the

bloom is open full the very soul shall be laid

bare. Know that every beat of my heart and

every breath is a sigh of love.

Carolee O'Neill

An Irish Tale

Dedicated to

loving grandparents

38

With God in Mind

Himself

The inside of the dark-green Hudson had tan door panels that were soft to Jennie's touch. As a little person of three, she loved to feel the velvety texture when she went with her grandpa. The windows had to be cranked open with a lever to make them go up and down though, a tough job for anyone other than an adult. She tried once or twice but could hardly get it to budge. It probably was for the best because at the speed they were traveling, she would stay put in the car if they met with an unfortunate mishap.

Jennie's head continued to swivel back and forth with the passing of trees, houses and people. Her grandpa always did his level best not to be late, even if it meant greeting Saint Peter at the Pearly Gates before his time. Getting a speeding ticket didn't enter his mind and somehow he seemed to sense where the officers were getting their coffee.

Far down the lane, a red light glowed softly through the haze of the morning mist. Jennie wondered if her grandpa would be able to stop in time or just continue through in hopes that it would turn green before skid-marks proved their passage.

Jennie had a hard time figuring out what her grandpa might be late for. She could understand being late for church, the priest would surely scold; and for the ice cream parlor— you could never be early enough for that. Of course, he couldn't make grandma wait or she'd get in a huff, in a loving sort of a way. Certainly, everyone agreed—once he got behind the wheel of the car, his mannerisms kinked. This mood prompted language that Jennie never heard in her parents' household, followed closely by a growl that surely came from his toes as his fist thumped on the steering wheel. Sometimes Himself would flip to other extremes, like driving to the edge of a mountainous cliff to see the valley far below while his passengers hung on for dear life; or when he'd
pass a semi, forcing an oncoming one onto the shoulder and then raise his fist at both of them.

When Herself was along, she'd ride in the

back seat and pray her rosary. Needless to say, she got very good at this. Jennie soon learned to ignore his actions—he was still her grandpa so she considered it part of the ride.

The destination often came as a surprise to Jennie and that didn't matter. She loved to go anywhere with her grandpa because most of the time there was a surprise at the end of the journey.

The park had swings where he'd push her high, a merry-go-round that made her sick and a slide so far above the ground her tummy tingled when she climbed the ladder. In any case, he always stood in just the right spot to give her the best of Himself.

Himself believed in everything good, even though Herself wouldn't agree. The race track comes to mind, first. When he'd take Jennie, he'd take her to the stables and teach her about horse-flesh. While she listened, she munched on a triple decker ice cream cone and picked her winner, which inevitably won, to his dismay.

Due to this hobby, time after time he'd find Himself in the hoosegow, along with one of his grandsons. Herself would bail out the child victim and leave Himself to ponder his behavior.

A good cigar floated between his fingertips as he gently tapped it on the edge of the ashtray that Herself kept spotless. Reading the racing form and playing with Jennie kept him out of Herself's way when he wasn't busy with his clients' insurance needs.

Jennie was sure that Himself had a pinch of leprechaun in him, most noticeably when he pulled pranks on Herself like the time he told her that his sister was coming to visit when she really wasn't. Herself ripped the house apart from the top of the long window curtains to the basement floor because Aunt Mae had a reputation for being mighty particular.

When the hour drew late, Herself asked Himself when he expected his sister to arrive. On that note, Himself almost swallowed his cigar.

The message was clear: if you weren't already leaving the room, the time had come to do so. Herself held a cast iron pan in her raised hand, moving fast toward Himself.

Nonetheless, Grandma didn't hit Grandpa with the pan. Himself was down on his knees, begging her forgiveness.

Looking down at him, Herself's grimace turned into an appreciative smile. She chuckled to Herself and thought, *maybe next time—unless the good Lord'll be by me side and me angel be perched on me shoulder because with the antics he pulls, that'll probably be tomorrow.*

Demons of the Mind

Ps 119: 169. Let my cry come
near before Thee, O Lord. Give
me understanding according to
Thy Word.

With God in Mind

The year passed with only the remembrance of pain, the kind that grips your heart and squeezes it dry.

You remember what it feels like don't you Lord. You experienced more pain in your earthly body than I could imagine. How it must have hurt when the cherubim who sat next to your throne turned traitor—and when those on earth whom you cared for cried, "Crucify Him!" You had shown them nothing but love. Do I feel a tear in your eye when I consider it?

You understand, don't you Father?

I don't need to tell you that there are demons in my head that replay recordings of conversations with the same despicable scenes. Trying to stop them I shout, "Get behind me Satan in the name of Our Lord, Jesus Christ."

Carolee O'Neill

They leave me briefly, but return within
the hour to haunt me with their redundant tunes,
using harsh words spoken by loved ones to cut
deep into the soul. They offer no relief! Their
indelible recordings remember the words well,
storing them on top of the rest of the loathsome
memories to create their masterpieces.

Where can I hide—in the words of friends?
Too often, friends offer consolation, but then the
mood is swallowed by a lecture.

Could I hide in the cheers of a football
game or a love song that speaks of what might
have been? Or could I use meaningless tasks to
sidetrack the thoughts. No, the robotic chores of
every day life only add to the rhythm of their beat
as more and more of my human side collapses to
countless recollections. You are my only hope.

With God in Mind

You understand, don't you Father?

Meekly I seek the power of your Holy
Spirit to drive the demons from my mind. I'm
weary of the hateful thoughts and cruel songs of
revenge, playing again and again. The demons that
tempt me laugh as I struggle against their sounds. I
beseech you Father, slash their grasp on my mind.
Make them cry out as I have had to do. Make them
lead their pain from my awareness. Force them to
swallow it unto themselves.

As always, a humble thank you does not
seem to be enough. But it comes from my heart.

Now it is finished!

I know, because you told me so in your
holy book.

All I had to do was ask, believing in what
you told me.

Thank you for listening and thank you for the peace of mind that you've sent my way. I know you did it, because . . .

You understand, don't you Father.

Standing Close

St. John: Chapter 17:24. "For
Thou lovedst me before the
foundation of the world."

Carolee O'Neill

As a wee spirit, I sat on your lap Father.
You told me a story about coming into the world
to do your work. I felt empowered. You
explained that I'd never be alone. You'd always
be at my side.

The earth parents that you placed me with
had me baptized in Jesus' name. The Holy Spirit
smiled. You were standing close. Many events
occurred before I understood what your story
meant. But as I grew up, I could see you in
everything. I marveled at how elegantly you
painted radiant colors into a sunset, how you
blackened the sky to show the brilliance of the
galaxies.

And when I talked to your trees, they
swayed with the wind and my body tingled from
their response.

With God in Mind

During Confirmation, my heart soared as
I pledged my loyalty to you for all eternity.
Every day was special, because I spent it with
you.

Then hardship overwhelmed my spirit,
again and again: too many evictions, ongoing
illnesses with the children, and no money for food.

You saddened when I blamed you.
Nevertheless, you stood close, holding me gently
in the palm of your hand.

You were patient as I walked through
adversity and waited as it led me back to you.

In desperation, my thoughts turned to the
Bible. The angels sang "Hallelujah" when I began
to study your word. You opened my eyes to the
truth as you fed this baby Christian the shepherd's
word.

Carolee O'Neill

As I grew with your love, I humbly bowed my head to your divine presence. Just as I sat on your lap as a wee spirit, I knew once again that everything was in divine order. Every day you would continue to light my pathway for the work you wanted me to do.

Now I go forth with joy because I know that you will always be standing close.

Published 2006: Together in Faith

The Hesitation

Ps 100: 2. Serve the Lord with gladness:
Come before His presence with singing.

Carolee O'Neill

It was late afternoon when I rounded the
corner heading for the bank. I began to ponder my list
of chores and noticed a small boy huddled against a
brick building, sucking his thumb.

Surprised, I hesitated.

Where is his mother or his father? Why is he
sitting there alone on such a busy walkway?

A pleading look crossed the child's face as his
eyes followed the individuals who passed by. Yet
everyone continued on their way, avoiding a glance
in his direction.

I can't believe that no one has the time to
stop.

I looked to the crowd for the answer, but
none came. The Christmas joy that lit my life
seconds before was gone. A pitiful sigh escaped
my throat, almost undetected.

It didn't matter that I didn't know his story. His probable fears caused me to feel an urgency to hold his small body and whisper words of comfort. I wanted to tell him how much his Heavenly Father loved him and that he didn't have to be alone. I wanted to tell him your story Father.

Just as I was about to go to him a lady grabbed my arm and warned, "Don't go near him. He might be contagious. His mother is."

I stared at her, shocked by her words. I turned back toward the child and for a brief moment, I hesitated.

What should I do? People depend on me to keep them well. I could carry a disease to them, if this child has one.

My heartstrings grew taut. *But if I turned my back on this child . . . Dear Father! What else would I be capable of doing? Wouldn't something deep inside change forever? And there wouldn't be an awareness of this, either. It would be like a tiny piece of shrapnel, breaking down my spirit, little by little. Then one day, I would no longer be a loving person. I'd be a person who had learned to ignore the needs of others.*

Could I then abandon my parents or my siblings and worse yet, turn my back on you Father?

I shuddered.

Instead, I'll ask for your protection in Jesus' precious name from any illness this child may have. I know you don't want me to spread disease to others.

With God in Mind

As I approached the child with an uneasy heart, his eyes captured mine. He began to sit up, slowly withdrawing his thumb from his mouth. A glimmer of his hope showered my soul when he smiled. Christmas joy leapt back into my heart as I took his little hand in mine.

"Come sweet child, you won't be alone any longer."

He jumped to his feet, embracing my legs as tight as he could. I glanced down into a dimpled face surrounded by a full head of curly, light-brown hair. As this child gripped my heart tighter than he could ever have gripped my legs, I knew that you put people in this world, so that they could ease the pain of loneliness, ease that feeling of abandonment—not just for children, but for all mankind.

Carolee O'Neill

Humbly Father, I ask that you forgive my
hesitation.

Your Child Calls

Ps 119: 169. Let my cry come near before
Thee, O Lord. Give me understanding
according to Thy Word.

Carolee O'Neill

Hear me my God!

Help me as you would your child.

Thousands of words rush through my head, searching

for how I became imprisoned within myself.

I feared the door to peace and contentment had

slammed shut in this lifetime.

Why have I been given so much only to have the

lines of talent severed with age and emptiness?

Out flowed the desire for accomplishment replaced

with loneliness and frustration.

My heart was heavy from the load.

Please don't let me wonder in the blackness of my

soul with no candle to burn.

Help me find an open door, so that I may

know true understanding within the depth of my

spirit. Then I can return to the child I once was

in my heart.

The Feeling of Candlelight

Ps 18:28. For Thou wilt light my candle. The
Lord my God will enlighten my darkness.

Carolee O'Neill

In the shimmer of candlelight, I ponder
joining my soul with the wind to sail the seas and
bond with the clouds to dwell in everlasting
softness.

With evening shadows fading, perhaps I
shall imagine how it would feel to grow as a tree of
many leaves or be a sea of rushing waters.

At dusk, my heart lies in a blanket of fog,
stilled by the silence of the valley.

I dream on.

My wonderings lead me to a quiet pond,
which reflects a full moon accented, by the star-
studded universe. I bathe in its completeness and
allow myself to unite with this world forever.

In time, will I have the eyes of a hawk by
day and those of an owl by night?

With God in Mind

These thoughts captivate my spirit and I dream on.

What would it be like to walk through a waterfall and not get wet or pass through a rainbow and taste its colors?

While I grasp these imaginings, I gently enfold my heart with peace and listen for my God.

It is certain that this heavenly dream goes beyond my understanding; yet my soul has led me to this place.

Enraptured by God's bountiful glory, I'm gently reminded that some say there is no paradise—there is no God.

The thought brings pain to my heart. I pray this is not true, for I fear the Lord will weep from the loss of their greetings.

Carolee O'Neill

As I ponder my journey to eternity and consider my beliefs, I wonder what these musings might suggest.

As a child of God, I shall cling to the idea that my heavenly crossover will be as easy as a bird hopping from one branch to another, quicker than the wink of an eye or faster than one beat of a humming bird's wing.

I place my faith in this passage so that when my time comes to enter my eternal home, it will be quicker than a match can light.

Yet, I will be spared from the pain of a burn or a blister, as I pass through the softness of candlelight.

by Carolee O'Neill, inspired by David.

Carolee

The author went back to college at age thirty-six, with five children at home, graduating magna cum laude. She practiced nursing in both large and small community hospitals that offered her a myriad of expertise. She then became an Infection Control Practitioner, which allowed her to orchestrate committee meetings, teach and lecture in the community for the hospital's Wellness Program. At eighty-two, her life is busy as an author, compiling her manuscripts, doing illustrations for her children's books, playing the piano, keeping up her home and garden, and traveling with her thirty-two foot motor home to promote her work.

With Warmest Regards,
Carolee

Carolee O'Neill

The Carolee Collectables

by Carolee O'Neill

Goodie RudeShoes: Series One, children 5 to 100.
Billy BitterBetter: Series Two, children 5 to 100.
Granny NeatFreak: children 4 to 100.
The Mouse House: children 4 to 100.
That Secret Part of Me: children 3 to 100.
From Silly to Sinister-Short Stories:
Book One and Two.
Fiction for teens through mature adults.
Navigating the Potholes of Life:
Fiction for teen and adult.
Adventure, comedy, drama.
A Reason to Dream:
Fiction for teen and adult.
Drama based on a true Story.
Three versions of The Graduation.
The Graduation: A stand-alone novel
for teens and adults.
The Graduation with Study Guide
for the parent with teens, teens and adults.
The Graduation Study Guide for
the person who prefers a separate copy of the guide.
Fiction: suspense, humor, insightful.
With God in Mind.
Thought provoking prose for
teens through mature adults.

caroleeagain1934@gmail.com
http://books2c4kids.com

Books are available as paperback and as ebooks.
Thank you for your interest in my work.

With God in Mind

Chocolate

*Book has been handcrafted from cover to cover,
including the watercolor illustrations by Carolee*

Carolee O'Neill

www.ingramcontent.com/pod-product-compliance
Lightning Source LLC
Chambersburg PA
CBHW070608180626
46817CB00005B/2052